BEMBELMAN'S BAKERY

Bembelman's Bakery

by Melinda Green
illustrated by Barbara Seuling

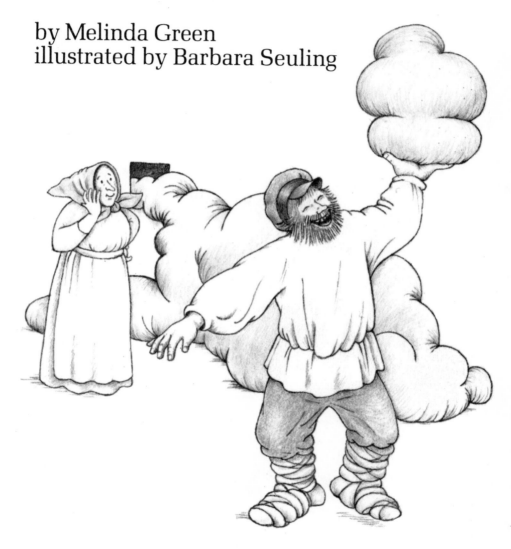

Parents' Magazine Press/New York

Printed in the United States of America
10 9 8 7 6 5 4 3 2 1

Library of Congress Cataloging in Publication Data
Green, Melinda.
  Bembelman's Bakery.
  SUMMARY: Relates the way in which Saul Bembelman
began baking bread.
  [1. Baking—Fiction. 2. Bread—Fiction. I. Seul-
ing. Barbara. II. Title.
PZ7.G8252Be [E] 77-22858
ISBN 0-8193-0913-3
ISBN 0-8193-0914-1 lib. bdg.

To Arlene, Wesley, Amy, David,
Eliott, Rebecca, and Benita Green
who are all hard workers

"**E**very time I walk past Bembelman's Bakery I see the same thing—lines. This Bembelman must be a great baker." "That bread he bakes is mostly luck, mister, let me tell you." "What do you mean, luck? He must be a genius!"

"Listen, there's a story behind this Bembelman. I come from the same village in the Old Country, and I know. It all began a long time ago, when we were both little boys...

Aaron Bembelman, the baker's father, was a hard worker.
He was a brickmaker, who made bricks eighteen hours a day.

His wife, Sarah Bembelman, worked just as hard at home.
They lived in a poor little house with hardly room enough for
their seven children. And they were a handful!

One day in late summer, Sarah had to go out to the market
to buy food for the harvest holiday that was coming.
She said to her oldest boy, "Saul, you watch the other
children while I'm gone, and don't get into trouble. Better
yet, don't even leave the house. I'll be home in two hours."
After Sarah went out, one of the children said,

"Saul, I'm hungry. And there is no bread in the house."
Saul thought for a minute.
"Then let's make some. We'll bake enough bread for today
and the holidays, too. Mama will be so surprised!"
"Yes! Yes! Let's make bread!" they all shouted.
"But how do we do it?" asked the youngest.

"I think Mama uses one handful of yeast," said Saul.
"But my hand is smaller than her hand. So I'll put in four
handfuls of yeast. And she uses six handfuls of flour."
"Are you sure?" asked Rachel.
"Yes," said Saul. "But my hand is smaller than her hand,
so I will put in more."

Then each of the children threw in a handful of this
and a handful of that and mixed it all together.

What a sight! Every little Bembelman was covered with flour
and sticky with dough. But finally, with a lot of pushing and
pulling, they got their mixture into the oven.

The dough began to rise and rise, and rise some more. Soon
it pushed out the oven door. When it reached the walls, it
began to push out the windows. Then the children got scared.
"What will happen when Mama comes home!" they cried.

So two hid under the bed, and one squeezed under the table.
One sneaked into the closet, and the other two sat huddled
together in the far corner. Saul stood by the door, trembling.
Bread was bulging everywhere—inside and outside!

And Rebecca Bergstein, the town gossip ever since she was three years old, ran to the marketplace yelling to Sarah Bembelman, "Oh, if you could see what your kids did to your house!"

"What!" screamed Sarah. "What have they done to my house?"

"You wouldn't believe me! You'll have to come see for yourself!" said Rebecca Bergstein.

Well, to make a long story short, there was yelling and
there was screaming, and there was praying to the Lord Almighty,
and Sarah Bembelman fainted three or four times when she saw
the house.

"Where are the children?" she hollered.

"They're all hiding," said Saul, peering out of the front door.

"When your father gets home," cried Sarah, "tired and hungry as he is, exhausted from his long day's work, he'll take each of you and teach you a lesson you'll never forget!"

As soon as Saul heard this, he ran to the woods to hide.

When Aaron Bembelman came home, the crowd parted to
let him through.

He sat down at his dining room table and, for a full fifteen
minutes, just stared in stony silence.

Sarah wept quietly in the corner.

Finally Aaron lifted his head and said, "So--- where is
dinner, Sarah?"

Sarah began to cry louder, and through her tears, she said,
"I can't get near the stove," "It is filled with bread."

Aaron sat silently for another five minutes. Then he said,
"So-- cut a piece of the bread."

The crowd peered through the dining room window.
Sarah gave Aaron a piece.

Aaron took a bite. He chewed it slowly. Then he smiled.
He took another bite and his smile grew wider. He ate some
more and began to laugh. Soon he was singing and smacking his
lips and dancing as he shouted, "Sarah, bring me more bread!

"This is not just bread," he cried. "Its meat and potatoes!
It's strudel and pie! It's breakfast, lunch, and dinner all at
once! It's apples and raisins, vodka and noodles, every taste
you ever wanted to taste, all in each wonderful bite."

The neighbors began crowding into the Bembelmans' house.
The bread was so good that they fought to taste it. Soon
Sarah began cutting off pieces the size of loaves, so that they
could take some home. The Bembelman children even crept
out of their hiding places to taste the bread.

Long after every crumb was gone,

the neighbors were still coming back, begging for more.

Sarah told them she'd have more by tomorrow.

Then she went to the woods to find Saul.

"SAULIE, MY DARLING !!!" she screamed at the top
of her lungs, "MAMA WON'T HIT YOU !!!
TELL ME HOW YOU MADE THE BREAD!"

There was a long silence.

Then, from somewhere in the woods came a voice.

"Well...You take ten handfuls of flour and four handfuls
of yeast..."

So the Bembelmans soon sold enough bread to come to America and open their bakery.

"And even now, nobody can bake bread like theirs. Who can copy a recipe that's measured by the hand-sizes of Bembelman children?

"So...come on. Let's get in line and buy a loaf."

"Why not wait until the line gets shorter?"

"It never gets shorter, believe me. Besides, I promised my grandchildren I'd bring them a bread from Bembelman's Bakery. And I'd better not come home without one!"

A recent graduate of Yale University, *Melinda Green* sang at Mory's with a women's vocal group, performed in dramatic productions, and drew cartoons for the *Yale Daily News*. While still a student, she was also a guest editor at *Mademoiselle*. *Bembelman's Bakery*—her first picture book—was inspired by stories she had heard as a child about her great-grandparents in the Old Country. The author grew up in Birmingham, Michigan, and now works in Chicago, Illinois.

A children's book editor for nine years, *Barbara Seuling* decided in 1973 to devote full time to writing and illustrating children's books herself. The artist, who grew up in Brooklyn, has been drawing ever since she was two years old. She studied at Hunter College, Columbia University and the School of Visual Arts. She now lives in Manhattan and is working, with other children's book authors and illustrators, on a project to help New York City's branch libraries.